TINY TOUGH

DORY
FANTASMAGORY

TINY
TOUGH

ABBY HANLON

Dial Books for Young Readers

For Margot

DIAL BOOKS FOR YOUNG READERS
An imprint of Penguin Random House LLC, New York

Copyright © 2019 by Abby Hanlon

Visit us online at penguinrandomhouse.com

Library of Congress Cataloging-in-Publication Data
Names: Hanlon, Abby, author, illustrator. | Title: Tiny tough / Abby Hanlon.
Description: New York : Dial Books for Young Readers, [2019] | Series: Dory Fantasmagory ; 5 |
Summary: "Dory's sure that her big sister's friendship troubles have to do with pirates, but she'll have to navigate those rocky waters without her imaginary first mate Mary, who's found an exciting new pal of her own."— Provided by publisher. | Identifiers: LCCN 2019008260 (print) | LCCN 2019011441 (ebook) | ISBN 9780525553991 (E-book) | ISBN 9780525553977 (hardback) | Subjects: | CYAC: Imagination—Fiction. | Imaginary playmates—Fiction. | Friendship—Fiction. | Brothers and sisters—Fiction. | Family life—Fiction. | BISAC: JUVENILE FICTION / Readers / Chapter Books. | JUVENILE FICTION / Imagination & Play. | JUVENILE FICTION / Humorous Stories. | Classification: LCC PZ7.H196359 (ebook) | LCC PZ7.H196359 Dm 2015 (print) | DDC [E]—dc23 | LC record available at https://lccn.loc.gov/2019008260

Printed in the United States of America
1 3 5 7 9 10 8 6 4 2

Designed by Jennifer Kelly
Text set in Albertina MT Std

TINY TOUGH

Dory's pirate name and her
walkie-talkie code name

Some Walkie-Talkie Lingo
That May Come In Handy:

Over = I'm done talking, now it's your turn.

Roger that = I understand.

Do you copy? = Did you hear me?

Over and out = Conversation over.

10-4 = I got your message.

CHAPTER 1
Such an Amazing Bath Toy

My name is Dory, but everyone calls me Rascal. I have a big sister named Violet and a big brother named Luke. They get all the attention and I don't get any! Except when they are busy after school. Then I get my mom all to myself. Because I'm never busy. Today my mom says we are going to the library. "Yay!" I say. "I can check out new books!"

"I love our afternoons together," says my mom. "You're my little partner."

"So that means you like me the best, right?" I ask.

She winks at me and says, "Nope."

At the library, I go straight to the big desk and ask the librarian, "You know that book about a family who eats breakfast in the shower and the mom wears a dress that's made out of live chickens?"

"And the boy eats with his feet and then the lights go off and they think they're dead but then their cat and dog turn on the electricity."

"Rascal, are you making this up?" asks my mom.

"No! It's a real book! And then they think they're in heaven but they're really in their living room? *It's so funny!* Do you have that book?"

"I'm sorry, I don't know that one," says the librarian.

"But here's a series you might like, it's called *Happy Little Farm*."

"That's okay, thanks anyway," says my mom. "Stop growling," she whispers, and leads me away from the desk.

My mom finds some books *she* likes and reads out loud. After seven books she says, "Rascal, I'm going to the bathroom. I want you to read quietly while I'm gone, okay?"

"I can't read."

"Yes, you can," she says. "I'll be right back."

A very short kid wearing a dinosaur tail starts talking to me. Her voice sounds like a frog. "Wead me it," she says, pointing to her book.

"I'm a bad reader," I whisper.

"I weally want you to wead it," she says.

"Ask someone else," I say.

"Wead it," says the kid.

"I guess I could tell you a story instead . . ." I suggest.

"I want a scawy stowy," she says.

"Well, that's easy . . . once upon a time . . ." I whisper, "well, actually right now, there lives a robber named Mrs. Gobble Gracker."

"Mrs. Wobba Wacka?"

"Yes . . . and she's very sneaky . . . She lives in a cave and she is 507 years old and has a big black cape . . . and . . . and . . . she has really long fingernails and FANGS like this . . . And she's been looking for me for a long time. *I am in great danger!* She wants to drag me off to her cave and pretend I'm her baby."

"I want to be in gweat danger," the kid says.

"Me too," says another kid.

"Are you scared?" asks a third kid.

"Of course I'm scared! But I have a monster and a fairy godmother who help me fight Mrs. Gobble Gracker. My monster sleeps under my bed. Her name is Mary, she is my best friend.

And my fairy godmother is named Mr. Nuggy and he can do magic. He lives in the trees and he has a big mustache, and once, a long time ago, he turned into a chicken. If I have an emergency, I can call him for help. I can call him from a banana."

Mr. Nuggy ↓

← Mary

Ring-Ring!

They have a lot of questions.

"SSHhhh!!! Be quiet, everybody! Mrs. Wobba Wacka woke up behind the couch!" says the girl with the dinosaur tail.

"What are you talking about? She sleeps in her cave!" I say. "And it's far away."

"She wants bweakfast!" she says.

"Quick, we gotta make it!" says another kid.

Then all the kids start making breakfast no matter what I say.

"If we don't make it faster, she'll throw bones at us," says one kid.

"I just saw a flying bone!" says another kid. "She's coming!"

"Oh no!" says a kid, diving into the couch.

"Well, you better have coffee," I warn them. "Mrs. Gobble Gracker drinks a lot of coffee in the morning."

"NO! She drinks *sauce*! Not coffee!" says a little boy.

"Bone sauce!" says the kid from inside the couch.

Then everyone hides from Mrs. Gobble Gracker.

Uh-oh. I see my mom coming back from the bathroom. I grab a book and pretend to read quietly.

"How's it going?" asks my mom.

The kid pops out of the couch.

CRUSH MRS. GOBBLE GRACKER!

"Dory—say good-bye. We're leaving," says my mom.

"But I didn't check out any books!" I say.

"I know, but I asked you to read quietly," she says. "And instead you've made all these kids savages."

"What's a savage?" I ask. My mom doesn't answer, she just walks quickly to the door. "Does it have something to do with pirates?" I ask her.

"I'm so sorry about the disruption," says my mom to the librarian.

On the way home, my mom says, "Rascal, I was thinking, well . . . you know how you outgrow things when you get older, like your shoes? Well, you might outgrow *other things* too, like . . . say . . . your Mrs. Gobble Gracker game, for example."

"I'm not outgrowing them," I say. "My shoes are shrinking."

"No, they're not," says my mom.

"Yes, they are!" I say.

"No, they're not," says my mom.

"Yes, they are!"

"You know, I just thought of something," says my mom, trying to change the subject. "What if we got you a new toy, *something really special.* Something that you might play with a lot, that might be even more fun than . . . your Mrs. Gobble Gracker game."

"Like a bribe?" I ask.

"Wha—no— Rascal! I would never—"

"Okay, I know what I want."

My mom looks happy. "What is it, honey?" she asks.

"TUBTOWN! I saw a picture of it in a magazine at Grandma's house. It's a town that sticks to the bathtub. It has suction cups that make it stick! It has an elevator! And a shower! And a fish and chips shop, and a lighthouse and a pool with a diving board and a little raft that the people can go in and float around the bathtub and—"

"Rascal, we already talked about this. That was a very old magazine. *You know how Grandma doesn't throw anything out* . . . The company doesn't make that toy anymore. I can't buy it."

"But that's impossible! They would never stop making *the best toy in the world!*"

TUBTOWN
SEASIDE VILLAGE

LIGHTHOUSE
Elevator Fish N Chips

BATH TOY
• attaches to side of tub
• safe and fun
• for kids ages two and up

"Well, they did," says my mom. "I already tried to buy it. It doesn't exist anymore."

"Does this have something to do with pirates?" I ask.

"Rascal—*did you understand any-thing I just said?*" asks my mom.

"When I get TubTown, I'm going to take a bath every single day. I'm going to smell clean as a dishwasher!"

"Rascal, can you be quiet now, I have to help Luke," says my mom.

Then she says a bunch of math stuff to Luke. Luke gets mad.

"I already know how to solve it!" he says. "You're interrupting me. I already did that step!"

"And I'm going to pretend that the little people in TubTown are all kids and they never grow up!"

"Luke, the answer can't be 64," says my mom. "That's not right."

"Yes it is!" says Luke.

"And they do backflips off the diving board," I say. "And they go head first down the slide into the ocean and they play in the waves all day!"

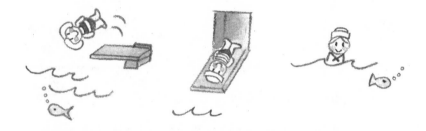

"Think about it," my mom says to Luke. "She can't have more cupcakes than she started with. You need to subtract. Can you just listen for one second—"

Luke wails, "First I added—*THEN* I subtracted!"

Violet comes in the kitchen. "Mom, I need to talk to you."

"Can you wait?" she asks Violet.

"No, I can't! I got in a huge fight with Anna today. She made friendship bracelets and she didn't make me one. But then I found one on my desk, and I thought she made it for me, so I put it on and she said that I stole it."

"A stolen bracelet?" I say, astonished. "Is it pure gold?" I ask.

"It's string. *Be quiet, Rascal!*" says Violet.

"Who's the thief?" I ask.

"There's no thief, Rascal," says my mom.

"Anna said she put it on the wrong desk—since everyone in my class just switched desks, she got confused," says Violet. "So, I told her she could have it back, but I couldn't get the string untied. When I finally got the string untied I was in the bathroom, so I put it in my pocket. When I got back to the classroom, it wasn't in my pocket! I told her I lost it, and she was really mad and didn't believe me."

"*A lost treasure?*" I ask. "Does this have something to do with pirates?"

"WHY ON EARTH DO YOU KEEP ASKING THAT?" yells my mom.

"Shush, Rascal!" says Violet.

"But I don't understand why Anna wouldn't make you a bracelet in the first place. She's your best friend!" says my mom.

"She said I was being bossy. But she's bossy too!" says Violet.

I grab a weapon.

Nobody calls my sister bossy!

"Put the broom down!" says my mom. "Come on, let's move away from Rascal." She leaves the kitchen with her arm around Violet.

"I can help you with your homework," I tell Luke.

"Yeah, right," he says.

"Just listen," I say. "If you have 64 cupcakes and you have 6 bags of pancakes, but if you sit on one bag of pancakes and 4 toucans go to the bathroom on your backpack, then how many bags of pancakes would you—"

My mom rushes back into the kitchen with
Violet trailing behind her. "Rascal, what happened? *Luke!* What did you do to her?"

"He flunjed me!" I cry.

"That's not even a word," says Luke. "She
was teasing me about my math. And I barely
touched her! She just fell."

"He flunjed me *really hard!*" I cry.

"She's just trying to get me in trouble!" says
Luke.

"Rascal, are you okay?" asks my mom.

I'm about to make a bunch of sounds like I'm in pain, and cry that Luke broke my butt— even though it doesn't really hurt *that* much. But then I notice that Violet's face looks red and splotchy.

She looks sad.

And I feel bad for her.

"I can help you solve your problem, Violet! Because I'm a pirate! And I'm the toughest!" I tell her.

So I stand up. I brush off my butt. And then at the top of my lungs, I yell,

"Oh no," says Violet. "Just when I thought my life couldn't get any worse."

CHAPTER 2
Something to Do with Pirates

"You know how I always walk into door-knobs?" I ask my mom the next morning.

"Uh-huh," she says.

"Well, it happened again. And now I need an eye patch!" I say, holding my hand over my eye.

"Your eye is fine," she says.

"How do you know? You didn't even look at it!" I say.

"Because I can tell when you are up to something . . ." she says.

"But I need an injury so I can look like a pirate!" I tell her.

"I'm sure you'll get hurt before the end of the day," she says.

"Can you punch me in the face and give me a black eye?" I ask Luke.

"Sure!" he says.

"*LUKE! NO!*" yells my mom.

"I wasn't really gonna do it," he says. "*I don't think . . .*"

After I don't get punched in the face, I look all around the house for a pirate jacket. I find one in Luke's closet.

"It's called a suit," says Luke.

"A pirate suit," I say.

"Pirates wear long jackets with shiny buttons, but I don't care, you can have it. I hate it," says Luke.

And then I remember that bandana with bones on it that a dog left at our house once.

When I show my mom my pirate suit, she says, "I *guess* you can wear it to school. I mean, it's kinda weird, but it does fit you perfectly..."

"Please! Please!" I beg.

"Well, you do match for a change, and it's nice that it's actually clean." She asks my dad, "Honey, what do you think?"

"Fine, wear the suit, Rascal," she says.

I have time to play before breakfast, so I grab a wooden spoon and wake up Mary.

But Mary says she's not in the mood to duel. "But you always have to be in the mood for what I'M in the mood for," I say, and drag her out from under the bed.

"I want to play cards," she says.

"Fine, we can have a Go Fish duel," I say, and grab the cards. "I'll deal."

But trouble starts right away. First, Mary bites me because she said I was cheating. (I was.)

Then Mary says I peeked at her cards. And so she tried to bite me. But she bit HER arm by mistake—she thought it was MY arm.

Then Mary gets mad at me because she says I stole her cards when she wasn't

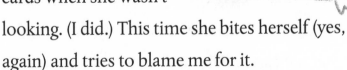

looking. (I did.) This time she bites herself (yes, again) and tries to blame me for it.

I grab the stolen cards and run downstairs.
Luckily, breakfast is ready.

"I'm going to help you find the treasure today,
and then Anna won't be mad at you anymore!"
I tell Violet.

"*It's not a treasure!*" says Violet. "It's a bracelet
made out of string! And it doesn't even matter.
Stay out of my business!"

"But I've got pirate business," I tell her.

"Aaaarrrrgghh! Give me toothpaste!!" I yell at Luke and Violet when we go to brush our teeth.

"You don't sound anything like a pirate," says Luke.

"Well then, how do I talk like a pirate?" I ask him. "What do pirates say anyway besides *Aaaaarrrgh*?"

I have a great idea.

"Well, you definitely asked the right people about pirates, 'cause we know," says Violet. "Right, Luke?"

"Aye, aye, matey," says Luke, with his mouth full of toothpaste.

"First of all, you have to talk in a gruff voice, move your hands around a lot, and talk really loud," says Violet.

"Okay!" I say.

"So, you know when pirates have to warn each other about danger—like if someone is firing a cannon at them?"

"Uh-huh," I say.

"They say, 'Lower down the cheese and crackers!'" says Violet.

"They do?" I ask.

"Yup. And wanna know what they say when they are really happy, like if they found a big treasure or something?" asks Luke.

"What?" I say.

"Ahoy, my big buttocks!" says Luke.

"More! Teach me more!" I say.

"Well, they never actually say 'walk the plank.' Someone just made that up. What they really say is, 'Spank the fishies!'"

"And you know about the pirate dance moves," asks Violet. "Right?"

"No." I shake my head.

"Don't worry, I'll teach you," says Violet. "This is what pirates do when they want to look extra tough. It's called the Macarena. Just follow me."

The Macarena

On the walk to school, I collect treasures in my treasure box.

I see a sparkly treasure and try to pick it up.

But when I get to school, nobody knows I'm a pirate.

My teacher says, "That's an interesting outfit, Dory."

"Thanks," I say. "I like your shirt . . . but not your skirt."

I have two best friends in my class. George and Rosabelle. I used to sit in between them, but my teacher said we talked too much, so she moved me next to Albert.

Albert and I fight every day because he is The Eraser Thief. Any time I have an eraser from home, he tries to steal it. But not today! Because I licked my eraser so he wouldn't take it. He got so mad at me, he said that my bandana makes me look like a camel. I don't even care one bit about looking like a camel!

Albert always says "This is so easy!" about everything. I hate when he says that! "This is so easy!" he says about our math problem. "The answer is 12."

"There are infinity answers," I tell him.

"You're wrong," he says.

"Nope, I'm right," I say.

After math, just as we are getting ready for reading, there's a loud crash in the classroom. "That was fun!" says George. Because that's what he always says when he gets hurt. But this time he bursts into tears.

"I bumped my head," he cries. "Ouch!"

"How did you trip, George?" asks the teacher.

"Look! His shoelaces are tied together!" says Rosabelle.

Rosabelle unties his laces but it takes a long time. "I'm trying!" she says. "But he triple knotted them!"

"That is not at all safe, George. Please don't ever do that again," says the teacher. "Dory, you can take George to the nurse."

The nurse asks George a bunch of questions. Then she tells him to lie down.

To get George to stop crying, I talk like a pirate.

I guess George isn't in the mood for pirates, because he just looks confused and keeps crying.

So I tell him all about TubTown, The Most Amazing Bath Toy Ever Invented. Finally, he stops crying! He wipes his tears and says, "I really really really want you to get TubTown." George is the greatest friend on earth. When I feel this way, I like to tickle him.

"Raise your hand if you really want me to get TubTown!"

When George is laughing, I notice his toes wiggling out of his socks. His sock has a hole so big that I can see two and a half toes.

"Hey, can I have that sock?"

"Sure, I don't need it," he says, and takes it off.

I smell it first—it doesn't  smell too bad for a sock. Actually, it smells kind of good. Like French toast.

I put the sock on my arm and stick my fingers right through the hole to make a cast. "Do I look like I broke my arm in a pirate fight?" I ask.

"Yeah," he says. "You look tough!"

"Stuff it with tissues to make it thicker," says George.

As I'm stuffing my cast with tissues, I hear a familiar voice at the water fountain right outside. It's Anna! And Hazel, Violet's other friend.

"I brought my string so we can make more friendship bracelets at recess," says Anna.

"I brought mine too!" says Hazel.

I stare at the friendship bracelets on their wrists.

"What if Violet finds out about the sleepover tomorrow night?" asks Hazel. *Violet?* They're talking about Violet! I listen harder.

"I'll feel really bad if she finds out," says Anna. "I've never had a sleepover without her . . . maybe we should invite her?"

"No! Don't worry, she won't find out!" says Hazel. "Wanna be partners on the next class trip?"

"Sure," says Anna.

They walk away and I can't hear them anymore.

"I gotta go," I tell George. Then I run out of the nurse's office and sneak up the back stairs to the big kids' hallway.

I have to help Violet! I have to tell her about the secret sleepover!

"Excuse me. Can I talk to Violet?" I ask Violet's teacher. "I live in the same house as her."

50

Violet doesn't look happy. "Why do you have a sock on your arm?" she asks.

"George said I could have it. Smell it—it smells like French toast!"

"No," she says, "I'm not smelling it. What are you doing in my classroom?"

"I need to tell you something . . ." I whisper. "I was at the nurse's office and I . . . I . . . um . . . heard . . . Aaa—Aaa . . ." Then I think, if I tell Violet what I heard about the sleepover, she might cry. And *if Violet cries, I'll cry.*

"Heard *what?*" she asks impatiently.

"I heard . . . a loud crack," I whisper.

"Huh?"

"My arm bone," I say, pointing to my cast.

"Why are you lying? Do you want me to tell mom that you are lying again?"

"Wait—" I don't want her to walk away. But for the first time in my whole life, I don't know what to say. "Um . . . um . . ." And then I say, "Breakfast was really good this morning, don't you think?"

"Rascal! Are those clothes making you act weirder than usual? What do you want?"

"I . . . I . . . need to ask you a very important question," I say.

"*Okay—what?*" she says.

I look down at my sneakers and ask the first

question that pops into my head. "You know the old lady who lives in the shoe?" I ask her.

"The nursery rhyme?"

"Yeah. Is the lady *really small* . . . or is the shoe *really big,* because I never understood, which one is it?"

"THAT'S what you wanted to ask me?! Get out of here, Rascal!"

CHAPTER 3
Starletta

After school, I pull off my bandana and yell at my mom, "Why did you let me wear these dumb, hot, scratchy clothes? *Nobody knew I was a pirate!* Everybody kept looking at me!"

My mom opens my backpack. "Don't tell me you lost your lunchbox again," she says.

"I did? Oh NO!" I cry. "It was full of all my treasures! Now they're gone!"

"Dory, you can't keep losing your lunchbox! You have to start keeping track of your stuff. That's part of growing up."

"I'm not growing! It's not even my birthday! *It's never my birthday!*" I pick up George's sock from the floor and throw it as hard as I can. I didn't know it was going to hit my mom's neck.

"That's it, Rascal! Go to your room," she says. "I need a break from you."

"I just got home!" I cry.

At least I always have Mary.

But as soon as I walk in my room, Mary grabs a banana to call Mr. Nuggy. "Rascal is covered in bumps! Come quick!!!" she yells.

What? I am?

"*Mary!*" I yell at her. "No I'm not! Why'd you say I'm covered in bumps? Why'd you prank call Mr. Nuggy?"

I grab the banana. "Hi, Mr. Nuggy, sorry about that—it's not really an emergency . . . there are no bumps. *No bumps!* Hello? . . . Hello? Are you there?"

I guess he already hung up.

Mr. Nuggy usually arrives pretty quickly after I call him.

Here he comes now!

Hee-hee!

"*Who are you?*" I ask.

"I'm Starletta," she says.

"What are you doing here? This doesn't make any sense. I didn't imagine you."

"Mary did," says Starletta.

"*Mary!?*"

"Stop jumping and listen to me! I imagine stuff and you go along with it! That's how this works!"

"I want my own imagination," Mary says. "You always get to imagine everything—and you're kinda bossy sometimes..."

"But I'm your best friend," I say.

"I know. But she's my wish come true..."

"What's so great about her?" I ask.

"I don't know yet . . . but I like how she looks like she always wants a hug," says Mary.

Hugs are gross.

"Wait a minute—where is Mr. Nuggy?" I ask Starletta. "Why did you answer his phone?"

"Oh, I was just floating around the sky, and I heard it ringing and ringing and ringing, so I answered."

"Hmmmm . . . that's strange," I say. "Where could he be this time?"

Hmmmm . . .

"So, who wants to go on an island vacation with me?" asks Starletta.

"*An island vacation?* Yes! Yes! I want to!" says Mary. "Let's go!" she says to me.

"NO WAY!" I say. "I'm NOT coming!"

"Why not?" asks Mary. "You have to come!"

"Because you and me are a two-person game, that's why!"

"But we can all be friends together," says Mary. "All three of us!"

I think of Violet and Anna and Hazel. "No, we definitely CANNOT!" I tell her.

That's when I remember . . . the brownie! I saved a brownie from school to cheer up Violet. "Hold on, I'll be right back."

I run to Violet's room.

"Ouch. That hurt."

Violet is holding her doll Cherry. *I thought she didn't care about Cherry anymore?* And she's crying. It's not loud crying like I cry. It's quiet crying, like Snow White. Snow White Crying is much sadder than my crying. I wonder if she knows about the secret sleepover?

"I didn't find your treasure . . ." I tell Violet. "But there was a birthday in my class today and guess what? We had brownies! And I saved mine for you! And it was the biggest!"

"Really?" she says, wiping her tears. *"You did? Where is it?"*

I try and get it out of my pocket, but it's extra gooey and kind of melted and sort of crumbly.

"It's in your *pocket*? Yuck!" says Violet. *"GET OUT OF MY ROOM NOW!"*

When I see Luke in the hallway, he looks at me and then starts screaming at the top of his lungs. "MOM!!! RASCAL HAS POOP ALL OVER HER HANDS! HURRY! I'M NOT LYING! SHE'S HOLDING POOP!"

"It was a brownie for Violet," I say, licking my fingers.

"Wash your hands," says my mom. "Actually, just take a bath. When was the last time you took a bath anyway?" I follow my mom around, crying.

"Rascal! I cannot get it! We've already discussed this *many times*! It's too old."

"Then let's just ask old people! They'll know! Where did all the TubTowns go?"

"People threw them away, they broke, some people probably still have theirs. But we can't buy it."

"People threw them away? *They threw TubTown in the garbage?* I don't believe you! Nobody did that!"

"Rascal, I'm done with this conversation. Get in the bath. And this time, please remember to take your socks and underwear off BEFORE you get in the bath. Socks and underwear are not body parts."

As my mom heads downstairs, I hear the front door open. Then I hear what sounds like a lot of loud and salty pirate boots stomping up the stairs, and my whole house smells like fish.

They pick me up and carry me out the door.

"This is so fun, guys, thanks for inviting me, but my family is probably wondering where I am . . ."

"Your mom said she needs a break from you," says the big pirate.

Well, she didn't mean **this!**

"You lost your lunchbox again, didn't you?"
asks the little pirate.

"Yeah, so what?"

"So, now you have to do our chores," says
the hairy pirate.

"Can I go home and get Mary first?" I ask.
"And my nightgown?"

"Get to work!" yells the little pirate.
And so I do.

I have to make
the pirates' dinner,

wash their feet,

... and walk
on their backs.

Then I have to scrub the decks.

Is that Mary I see out the window? MY Mary?

I run to the upper deck.

She went on vacation without me! And she's with that pointy-head dumb-dumb?

Jealousy hits me like a giant wave, dragging me under, spinning me around and around, water up my nose, sand in my eyes. Everything is salty.

Now I know how Violet feels.

I wave my hands and yell, "Mary! Mary! Over here! Help!"

But she is too far away. She doesn't see me. She can't hear me.

"NO! NO! NO!" I cry. "Mary can't have another friend! I'm the only one!"

"Looks like even Mary wants a break from you," says the big pirate.

"Wow! Nobody wants you!" says the little pirate.

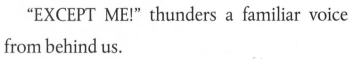

"EXCEPT ME!" thunders a familiar voice
from behind us.

CHAPTER 4
Long Bones

"*Mrs. Gobble Gracker!* What are you doing here?" I ask her.

But she doesn't have time to answer that. One by one, she has to fight each pirate.

And one by one, she throws them overboard.

"Time to get out of here!" she says. We jump off the pirate ship into her little getaway boat.

"Since when are you a pirate?" I ask Mrs.
Gobble Gracker.

"I needed to get out of my cave," she says.
"Since when are you—what are you supposed
to be in that outfit? A lawyer?"

"No! Ugh! I was trying to help Violet find a
treasure and—oh, forget it."

"Treasure?! That's what I'm looking for!"
says Mrs. Gobble Gracker.

"What a coincidence," I say.

"Don't say big words," she says. "Say goo goo ga ga."

"Why?"

"'Cause I finally caught you. So that means YOU ARE MY BABY! Ha-ha-ha! Ha-ha-ha!"

Oh brother.

"Coochie coochie coo," says Mrs. Gobble Gracker. "We're going to make a great team!"

"Maybe we will," I grumble. "Maybe I'm just as bad as you after all . . ."

"All this time, I always knew we belonged together," she says. We get out of the rowboat and climb aboard Mrs. Gobble Gracker's ship. I recognize Mrs. Gobble Gracker's helpers from a long time ago.

"Follow me to the dressing room," she says,
"where we will find your baby pirate outfit."

When I come out of the dressing room, Mrs. Gobble Gracker squeals with delight. "You look so cute! And I have the perfect baby pirate name for you. Are you ready?"

"Presenting . . . my very own: Tiny Tough!" she says.

"Tiny Tough? Hmmmmm . . . yeah, I kinda like that," I say.

For dinner, Mrs. Gobble Gracker feeds me baby food.

"I haven't had this in a while. It's actually pretty good," I say, and open my mouth wide.

"Mmmmmmm," says Mrs. Gobble Gracker, feeding me.

"So, let me get this straight—you don't want me to grow up, right?" I ask Mrs. Gobble Gracker. "That means no chores and I can lose all my stuff?"

"That's right, 'cause you're my little baby," says Mrs. Gobble Gracker. "And I love *my little baby.*"

"So you'll always love me . . . no matter what I do?" I ask, and drop my spoon. 'Cause that's what babies do.

"I'll love you forever, no matter what," she says, and picks up the spoon.

"But what if you're dead?" I ask, and drop the spoon.

"I'll still love you when I'm dead," she says, and picks up the spoon.

"But what if I kill you?" I ask, and drop the spoon.

"Hee, hee, hee," I laugh. *Just kidding.*

After dinner, Mrs. Gobble Gracker says she has a baby monitor for me—so she can always know where I am.

"Mrs. Gobble Gracker, this is a walkie-talkie," I tell her. "You know that, right?"

"Oh, whatever," she says. "I can't keep up with all this technology."

I teach her some walkie-talkie lingo.

"What's your code name?" I ask. "Mine is Tiny Tough, of course." Mrs. Gobble Gracker picks "Long Bones."

"Not a bad choice," I tell her.

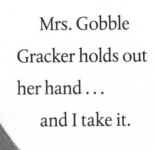

Mrs. Gobble Gracker holds out her hand . . .

and I take it.

On our first adventure together, we sneak up on a ship of rich ocean cats and steal their gold.

We're bad. *Really bad!*

After that, it was clear. We were a great team.

Mrs. Gobble Gracker	me
☑ big	☑ big muscles
☑ scary	☑ fast
☑ sword-fighting skills	☑ smart
☑ highly motivated by greed	☑ can hide in small places
☑ has pirate gear	☑ can do the macarena

I hear my mom yelling, "Rascal! Get out of the bath! What on earth are you doing in there for so long? First you won't take a bath, then you won't come out!"

"Stop talking to that bar of soap. And why is there so much water on the floor?" she yells, slipping on the bathroom tile.

"There were a lot of big fights in here," I say.

That night at dinner I tell my family that I don't think my nickname should be Rascal anymore. "Because what does that even mean? Nobody knows!"

"It means troublemaker," says Luke. "Duh."

"*It does???* *Heeeeeyyyyyy!* MOM?!"

"Not in a bad way, in a loving way," says my mom.

"I want a new nickname! From now on, just call me . . . Tiny Tough!" I say, and flex my muscles.

Luke spits out his drink, laughing. "Nobody is going to call you that," he says.

"Mrs. Gobble Gracker does," I say.

"You're *friends* with Mrs. Gobble Gracker now?" Violet laughs.

I hate it when they laugh at me and I don't know why. "Not exactly friends . . ." I say. "More like business partners."

"So, you've crossed over to the dark side?" asks Luke. "Like in *Star Wars?*"

"Once you start down the dark path, forever will it dominate your destiny," says my dad.

Later that night:

I find out that Mrs. Gobble Gracker cannot handle having a walkie-talkie. She keeps hitting the TALK button without realizing it. I hear her say a lot of weird stuff. *What is she doing?*

"This is Tiny Tough to Long Bones. Do you know you keep pushing the TALK button? Can you please stop? I have to go to bed. Do you copy?"

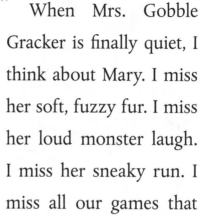

7:42 p.m.

WHOOPS! Sorry about that. Lullaby and good night. Over and out.

When Mrs. Gobble Gracker is finally quiet, I think about Mary. I miss her soft, fuzzy fur. I miss her loud monster laugh. I miss her sneaky run. I miss all our games that we play. I even miss when she gets mad at me and goes bonkers and sits on top of me. I wonder what she's doing right now. And when is she going to come home?

How do you fall asleep when you don't have a monster under your bed?

CHAPTER 5
Sock Muscles

The next morning I put socks in my shirt so it looks like I have big muscles. Rosabelle and George love my muscles. "Just call me Tiny Tough," I tell them. "That's my pirate name."

"Let's pretend I'm a pirate princess!" says Rosabelle. "And we live on a little island together!"

"Arrgh!" I say.

"And let's pretend a bottle floated to our island with a treasure map inside!" Rosabelle adds.

"And we have to go on a treasure hunt," I say.

"I'll make a treasure map!" she says, taking out her notebook.

"Can I be your parrot?" asks George.

"Yes! But since you're a parrot," she says, drawing the map, "you have to copy whatever I say, 'cause that's what parrots do."

"Squawk! Squawk!" George says in a super high screechy parrot voice. He flies around the schoolyard and crashes into the fence.

"That's not copying me, George!" yells Rosabelle. "Get back here right now!"

That morning, our teacher says we are going to learn a new song for math today. It's about counting money. She sings, *"Penny penny, easily spent, copper brown and worth one cent."* And we sing it back. But George sings in his super high, screechy parrot voice. The teacher says, "Who's singing in that awful voice? Whoever that is, please stop."

We sing, *"Nickel nickel, thick and fat, you're worth five cents, I know that."*

"George, is that you? Sing in your regular voice, please!" says the teacher.

In his super high, screechy parrot voice, George says, "Sing in your regular voice please!" All the kids burst out laughing. Rosabelle whispers to me, "NOW he decides to copy?"

"George! That is not funny! You are not allowed to sing anymore!" says the teacher.

Then we go back to our desks so we can work on counting money. "Sit nicely, and the math helpers will pass out the plastic coins," says the teacher.

I write my new name on my math paper.

"This is so easy!" says Albert. "I could count money when I was three."

Name: TINEETUF
Use your coins to make
9 cents

12 cents

23 cents

51 cents

"When you were three, I bet you looked like a baked potato," I tell him.

When I see the coins, I get very excited. I mouth the words to myself, *"All the treasure in the world is mine."*

penny
1¢

nickel
5¢

dime
10¢

quarter
25¢

At first I just sneak a few coins from Albert when he isn't looking. But once I get the greedy and all-powerful feeling of being super rich, I sneak around the classroom and rob handfuls of money off the tables.

I use one of my sock muscles as a money bag.

"Dory, we're *counting* the money, we aren't *playing* with it!" the teacher says. "And if you don't stop *playing*, you're going to have to miss recess . . . again."

Rosabelle grabs me by the shoulders. "Tiny Tough," she whispers. "You CANNOT miss recess today . . ." Now she's talking in her dead serious voice. ". . . because a group of really mean pirates came to our island! They stole my treasure map, and they tied me up! And YOU have to rescue me!"

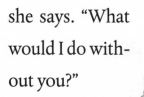

"I think I know those pirates . . ." I say.

"You're the only one who can save me!" she says. "What would I do without you?"

Here you go.

I don't know how to tell time, but I quietly stare at the clock anyway. Because I can't wait for recess.

Finally:

Recess was more fun than ever.

After school, I see Violet alone. And then I see Anna with Hazel together on the other side of the schoolyard.

I march up to Anna. She smiles at me and says, "Hi, Rascal, what's up?"

I show her my muscles and in my gruffest pirate voice I yell, "IT'S TIME FOR YOU TO SPANK THE FISHIES!"

And then I do
the Macarena.

Why are they giggling? This is a disaster.
Now what do I do? I feel like dying. So I pretend
to stab myself in the heart. I close my eyes and
make disgusting dying noises and fall over.

"Is she okay?" asks Hazel.

"Yeah, she's fine," says Anna.

"I'm dead," I say.

"Then why are you
talking?" asks Anna.

I think about
this for a second.
Then I jump up and run away.

Luckily, Violet doesn't see any of this.

On our walk home, I tell Luke and Violet that George isn't allowed to sing anymore and all about stealing the fake money.

"So you almost missed recess … for stealing *fake money?*" asks Luke.

"Yup," I say. "But don't tell Mom."

"If there is anyone in this world who would steal fake money, it would be you, Rascal," says Violet. "Actually … I kinda like that about you."

CHAPTER 6
Opposite Day

As soon as I get home, I grab my walkie-talkie. "Tiny Tough to Long Bones—please state your location."

"Meet me at Monkey Island," she says. "Use the map I left under your pillow, over."

"10-4," I say.

On Monkey Island, we dig for treasure. But the monkeys keep throwing coconuts at Mrs. Gobble Gracker. "Why aren't they throwing them at you?" she yells.

"Because everybody loves Tiny Tough," I
say. But when I look through her telescope,
I don't feel so good anymore.

Mary and Starletta are snorkeling together.

I sit by the edge of the water and cry. A large fish tail splashes out of the water.

Wait, it's not a fish . . .

"Mr. Nuggy! You're here!" I yell. *"Are you a mermaid?"*

"No!" he says. "It's Opposite Day! So I turned my feet into a tail and ate dinner for breakfast! And then I thought, what the heck—I'll just wear this bikini and go for a swim."

"I love Opposite Day!" I say. "I mean—I hate Opposite Day!

"Guess what?" I tell him. "I'm a baby and Mrs. Gobble Gracker is my partner!"

"Ha-ha-ha! That's a great idea for Opposite Day! I mean, a terrible idea!"

"No, I'm serious! I mean, I'm not serious!"

"Okay, Mr. Nuggy, don't listen," I say. "I don't need your help at all."

"I'm not listening," says Mr. Nuggy with a twinkle in his eye. "Not one little bit."

"Mary has a REAL friend," I say slowly. And in my angriest voice I say, "And I'm sooooooo HAPPY about it." Then I ask, "Can you not do a spell on Mary to make her imagination BIGGER*?"

"Nope," he says, smiling. "I definitely can't do that."

"Don't do it now! She's not over there!" I yell, and point to her in the water.

Then I climb up the ship's mast so I can get a better view of Mr. Nuggy's magic.

*Non–Opposite Day Translation: "Can you do a spell on Mary to shrink her imagination?"

"Aaaahhhhhh! Oh my gosh, you scared me! Get down right now! What on earth are you doing on top of the refrigerator?" gasps my mom.

"I'm on top of Mrs. Gobble Gracker's pirate ship!" I tell her.

"And give me that baguette!" she says.

"And I can see everything from up here!"

"You know, Rascal, if I knew that you would behave this way, I would have told George's parents that you are NOT grown up enough for a sleepover."

"*Sleepover?* Did you say *sleepover?*"

"George's parents have to go to a party and their babysitter canceled, so I told them that George could sleep here tonight. But now I really—"

"*Tonight? My first sleepover! I'll behave!*"

"Okay, *then show me*," says my mom.

But as soon as my mom leaves the room . . .

"You're my baby forever—remember?" says
Mrs. Gobble Gracker. "I'm taking you right back."

"If you don't let me go, I'll never get to see
George in his pajamas! And I bet he's going
to wear his volcano pajamas! I just know it!
'Cause they're his favorite! He always talks
about them!"

Mrs. Gobble Gracker takes me back to the ship and wraps me up so tight in a blanket that I can't move my arms. I cry louder than any baby has ever cried.

Night falls. For a while everything is quiet. The ocean is still. The sky is full of stars.

When the sun rises, a little bunny hops inside my crib.

"Who are you?" I ask.

"I'm Mary's friend."

"*Mary's friend.* What's your name?"

"Mary didn't name me yet. Can you name me?" she says.

Before I can think of a name . . .

I see another bunny.

And then another one.

And then three more.

And then my crib is full of them. And then I see the entire ship is full of creatures that look sort of cute and sort of dumb.

"We're being attacked by I don't know what!" I hear Mrs. Gobble Gracker screaming. "Load the cannons!"

"Mary! You're here!"

"Rascal! Are you okay? I came as soon as I heard you were captured! And all my imaginary friends came to help!" says Mary.

Mary frees me from my blanket and I jump out of my crib.

"How did you get so many friends?" I ask her.

"I have no idea! I was snorkeling with Starletta, and I felt a little sparkly zap on my brain and then all of a sudden my imagination started exploding! I couldn't stop thinking of new friends!"

"Interesting," I say. "Hold on a second."

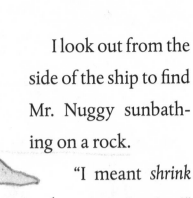

I look out from the side of the ship to find Mr. Nuggy sunbathing on a rock.

"I meant *shrink* her imagination!" I yell. "Remember? It's Opposite Day?"

I got confused. I'm sorry.

"It's okay," I say.

"Can we go home?" asks Mary. "I'm way too popular here!"

Yes!

"Next time, I hope you come on vacation too," Starletta says to me.

"I'll think about it," I say. I give her a hug, because, what the heck. She looks like she really wants one.

With Mary home, safe and sound and sitting on the toilet, I put on my nightgown and then run to tell Luke and Violet the big news. "Guess what! George is sleeping over! Tonight! And I know he's going to wear his volcano pajamas!"

"*You're* having a sleepover? *You?* Even my little sister is having a sleepover?" says Violet. A big tear rolls down her cheek.

Oh no! *She knows about the secret sleepover.*

"But you can play with us!" I tell Violet.

"When pigs fly!" says Violet. "That means never, by the way." And then she runs upstairs crying.

I wait at the window for George.

When Mary's friends fly by, I wonder . . . maybe Violet will have some sleepover fun after all.

CHAPTER 7
The Sleepover

Just when I think I'll die if I have to wait one more second, George arrives wearing his volcano pajamas. And he has on a giant camping backpack. My mom says, "Wow, George, it looks like you came *very prepared*."

"My parents said I could pack my bag by myself," says George.

"How *responsible* of you," says my mom, giving me a look.

"They were in a rush," he says.

The bag is so big
George has to crawl
up the stairs. I
help push
him up.

When we reach my room, I ask, "What did you pack? What's in your backpack? Open it!"

George pulls out one very large thing.

"A rubber sleeping bag?"

"No, it's a rubber raft. We can blow it up!"

"That's all you packed?"

"I couldn't fit the oars," he says.

"No clothes? No toothbrush? No underwear?" I ask him.

"I only wear underwear on special occasions," says George. "Now, guess why I brought this raft?"

"Ummm . . . In case my house has a big flood?"

"Nope, guess again."

"Because you pee when you're sleeping? So you need a waterproof bed? I won't tell anyone."

"NO! For TUBTOWN, you silly!!" he says. "You don't need to buy it because now we can just play it!"

Wow, George is the greatest friend in the whole universe.

We take turns blow-
ing up the raft. It takes
a long time.

We use up all the air inside us.

When we get our energy back, we put on
bathing suits and throw the raft down the
stairs. Then we carry it to the backyard.

We find big sticks to row with. "Row faster!"
George keeps yelling.

"We're almost there!" I say. "I think I see it!"

Eat fish and chips.

We go up the elevator.

Take a shower.

Slide head first.

Look out from
the lighthouse.

Jump off the diving board.

And then we have a visitor.

"Wow. This is nice and cozy," says Luke.

"Let's dump him out," I say.

"Violet, help me!" yells Luke.

"I need backup!"

Violet and Luke drag us out of the raft. But we keep running and jumping back in and they drag us out again. Everybody is laughing.

I don't know why, but George keeps calling Violet "Sergeant."

"Help! The Sergeant got me!" yells George.

"Stop calling me that," says Violet. "Although . . . it might be fun to be the Sergeant and boss you guys around."

"YES! Boss us around! Please!" I beg.

"Please, Sergeant!" begs George.

"I know! Let's play army boot camp!" says Luke.

"Okay," says Violet, "I want 50 push-ups from each of you."

Then my mom calls from the window, "Violet! Anna is on the phone."

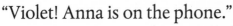

Violet runs inside.

We stop doing push-ups. I peek in the window and spy on Violet.

I can't hear what she is saying, but she is smiling.

I lie in the grass with Luke and George. "I guess this is the end of our game," says Luke.

But then Violet comes back . . . blowing a whistle! "YAY!" we all cheer. "The Sergeant is back!"

She makes us do jumping jacks and run around the yard.

After our warm-ups, the Sergeant says we are ready for our first challenge. We have to make all the beds in the house.

"No way! They don't make their beds in the army!" I complain.

"Of course they do!" yells the Sergeant. We try really hard. But when the Sergeant comes to inspect she says we all failed.

After dinner, we compete in our next challenge. It's called "Who Has the Most Will Power?" which means who can eat their chocolate pudding last. We all tie for last place. "I guess I'm the winner even though I wasn't even playing," says the Sergeant.

After our final challenge, an obstacle course in the backyard in the dark, we have an awards ceremony. Violet made awards for everyone!

I get third place.

Luke gets second place.

And George gets first place! The gold medal.

That night, George and I stay up late and eat cookies and nobody ever finds out.

The next day, Violet makes me a friendship bracelet.

And then she makes a whole bunch more. "Who are they for?" I ask her.

"I have a lot of friends," she says.

"Really?" I ask.

"Some real and some imaginary," she says. She winks at me and smiles.

THE END.

Don't miss the first four
DORY FANTASMAGORY books

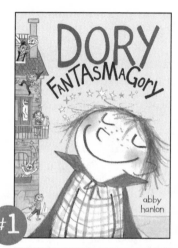

#1

#2

#3

#4

Abby Hanlon (www.abbyhanlon.com) is a former teacher. Inspired by her students' storytelling, she began to write her own stories for children and taught herself to draw. She is the author of Ralph Tells a Story and the Dory Fantasmagory series. The first, *Dory Fantasmagory,* was an ALA Notable Book, a *Kirkus, Publishers Weekly,* and *Parents* Magazine Best Book, and a Golden Kite Honor Book. The second, *The Real True Friend,* won a Cybil Award, and the third, *Dory Dory Black Sheep,* was an ALA Notable Book. Abby lives in Brooklyn, New York, with her husband and their two children.